my little sister

the beach

Sam's hou

2

Hi. My name is Sam.

This is my family.

Dad

Susie,
my little sister

Gran

Chapter 1
Knock over Blocks

Dad and I used to play blocks.
Then Susie came along.

Now Mum says, 'You boys make too much noise when you play with the blocks. You will wake Susie up!'

Susie is *always* asleep. But when
she is awake she knocks over my
biggest-ever block tower.

I tell Dad, 'Susie knocked over my biggest-ever block tower.' I tell him, 'Susie should be in **big** trouble.' But Dad says, 'Susie is just a baby. Make another tower Sam.'

But it will not be easy. How can I make the biggest-ever block tower *and* be quiet?

Chapter 2
Not the Shops

Mum and I used to have fun going to the shops. Then Susie came along.

Susie doesn't like going to the shops.

She cries as loud as she can.
Mum gives her *my* new red car
to stop her crying. But Susie is
breaking my new red car.

I tell Mum, 'Susie is breaking my red car.' I tell her, 'Susie should be in **big** trouble.' But Mum says, 'Susie is just a baby. We will buy you another car Sam.'

Susie should be in big trouble.

But I don't want another car. I am never going to the shops with Susie again.

Chapter 3
Hole in the Cone

Grandpa and I used to make
ice-cream cones. Then Susie
came along.

Now when we make ice-cream
cones Grandpa says, 'Let Susie have
a lick of your ice-cream Sam.'

Susie licks the ice-cream part
right off the cone part.

I tell Grandpa 'Susie licked the
ice-cream part right off the cone part.'
I tell him, 'Susie should be in **big**
trouble.' But Grandpa says,
'Susie is just a baby. We will make
another ice-cream cone Sam.'

Susie should be in big trouble.

But it won't be easy to make
another ice-cream cone. Susie has
bitten the ends off *all* the cones.

14

Chapter 4
Let Go!

Gran and I used to read stories.
Then Susie came along.

Now when we read stories Gran says,
'Let Susie read with us Sam.'

Instead of reading the book,
Susie pulls my hair.

I tell Gran, 'Susie is pulling my hair and if she doesn't stop, she will pull it out.' I tell her, 'Susie should be in **big** trouble.' But Gran says, 'Susie is just a baby. Your hair will grow again Sam.'

Susie should be in big trouble.

But when it does I won't be here. I am running away from home.

Chapter 5
Susie says 'Sam!'

Susie said her first word today.

Mum said, 'Did she say Mum?'
Dad said, 'Did she say Dad?'
Grandpa said, 'Did she say Grandpa?'
Gran said 'Did she say Gran?'

But Susie said 'Sam!' She said,
'Sam, Sam, Sam.'

I think Susie is in **big** trouble. But I say,
'Susie is just a baby. She will say your
name one day, but not right now
because ...

... Susie is making the biggest-ever block tower with me!'

Survival Tips

Tips for surviving your little sister

1   Lock up your blocks.

2   Don't try to make the biggest-ever block tower when your little sister is awake.

3   Lock your bedroom door.

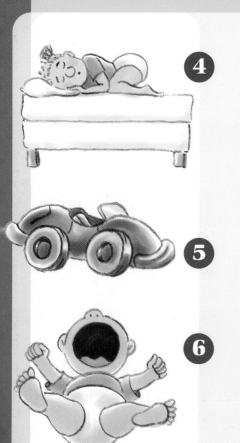

4 Be very quiet when your little sister is asleep. The longer she sleeps the less time she is awake and, the less time she can annoy you.

5 Lock away your new red car.

6 Have earplugs ready — little sisters cry a lot.

Riddles and Jokes

Sam My sister has long hair, all down her back.

Con Funny it's not on her head.

Little sister to shopkeeper.
    I would like a frog for my brother.
Shopkeeper to little sister.
    Sorry we don't do trade-ins.

Sam My sister cut a hole in her umbrella.

Con Why did she do that?

Sam She wanted to see when it had stopped raining!

Mum Sam why did you put a frog in your sister's bed?

Sam Because I couldn't find a spider.